Waltham Forest Libraries L

Please return this item by the last date stamped. The loan may be renewed unless required by another customer.

05/2019		

Th

Need to renew your books?
http://www.walthamforest.gov
Dial 0333 370 4700 for Callpoi   renewal
line. You will need your library
know your PIN, contact your l

D1363253

'The Little Green Monster'
An original concept by Jill Atkins
© Jill Atkins

Illustrated by Daniel Limon

Published by MAVERICK ARTS PUBLISHING LTD
Studio 3A, City Business Centre, 6 Brighton Road,
Horsham, West Sussex, RH13 5BB
© Maverick Arts Publishing Limited March 2019
+44 (0)1403 256941

A CIP catalogue record for this book is available at the British Library.

ISBN 978-1-84886-431-3

www.maverickbooks.co.uk

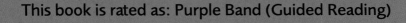

Purple

This book is rated as: Purple Band (Guided Reading)

The Little Green Monster

By Jill Atkins

Illustrated by Daniel Limon

Cosmo woke up early on the day of his Wizard Test. He was too nervous to eat his breakfast. So he polished his wand and had another look at his spell book. He wanted to make sure he could remember all his spells!

"Don't worry, Cosmo," said his dad. "You have learned a lot about being a wizard!"
"Yes," said his mum. "Just try hard and do your best. You will be fine!"
Cosmo still felt nervous as he set off for the test. But he kept going because he really wanted to be a wizard.

Cosmo went into the deep dark cave.

His hands were shaking and his knees were

knocking. Ms Fizz was already there.

"Are you ready?" she boomed. Cosmo nodded.

"So let's begin," said Ms Fizz. "You have

three tests."

The first test was written on top of a toadstool.

Cosmo smiled. It was easy.

He fetched some purple powder, some red glitter

and some magic dust. He mixed the potion in the

big cauldron. It started bubbling away.

"Well done!" said Ms Fizz. "Now for test

number two."

The second test was stuck to the cupboard.

Cosmo smiled when he read it. It sounded fun!

He put on his goggles.

Then he collected the right ingredients from

the cupboard. He made some brilliant spells.

They frothed and sparkled.

"Excellent!" said Ms Fizz.

Cosmo felt good. "I'm doing well," he thought.

"Now for the last test of all," boomed Ms Fizz.

"It's important that you get this one right."

Cosmo's tummy fluttered. He looked at the stone

in Ms Fizz's hand.

"Turn this stone into a mouse," boomed Ms Fizz.

Cosmo gulped.

"Remember this magic word," boomed Ms Fizz.

"SALLYLONGSHANKS."

"Sally… long… shanks," said Cosmo.

"Sallylongshanks."

"Good," said Ms Fizz. "Now don't forget it."

"Take five drops of the potion you made in your first test," boomed Ms Fizz. "Drip them onto the stone. Next, wave your wand and say the magic word."

"Yes, Ms Fizz," whispered Cosmo.

Ms Fizz swooshed out of the cave. Cosmo was on his own. Quickly, Cosmo ran to the cauldron and took five drops of potion. He carried the potion to the toadstool and dripped it onto the stone... one, two, three, four, five.

"Good so far," he muttered. "Now for the magic word."

"Sally..." He stopped. What was next?

"Sallylong..." He couldn't remember the ending! He waved his wand over the stone.

"Sallylong... socks," he said.

Sizzle! Hiss! Crackle! Bang! Flash!

Green smoke and sparks came from the stone.

"That was so clever!" Cosmo laughed.

"The spell worked brilliantly!"

When the smoke cleared, Cosmo got a shock.

Cosmo stood still. His mouth was wide open.

His hair stood on end. There was something very

odd sitting on the toadstool.

"What are you?" asked Cosmo.

"Ha ha!" it laughed. "I'm the Little Green Monster."

"Oh no!" cried Cosmo as the Little Green Monster

jumped down and scampered across the room.

"He he!" it giggled. "Can't catch me!"

"Come back!" called Cosmo, but he couldn't catch

the Little Green Monster.

The Little Green Monster knocked over a stool with a crash.

"Stop!" shouted Cosmo, but the Little Green Monster didn't stop. It ran over to Ms Fizz's desk and jumped up.

"Wheeeee!" it screeched. It tipped over a pot of glittery stars.

"Oh no!" Cosmo shouted again. "Ms Fizz will be back soon. She'll be cross and I'll be in trouble. Quick! Fetch a brush."

The Little Green Monster fetched a brush.

"Not a toothbrush!" said Cosmo.

The Little Green Monster fetched another brush.

"Not a hair brush!" Cosmo sighed.

The Little Green Monster fetched a third brush.

"Not a toilet brush!" Cosmo laughed. "I'll have to fetch the right brush myself."

Cosmo fetched the dustpan and brush and began to sweep up the stars. At that moment, Ms Fizz came back.

"Cosmo!" she boomed. "What's going on?"

The Little Green Monster hid under the cauldron.

Cosmo felt like crying as he looked at the mess.

'Ms Fizz won't let me be a wizard now,'

he thought.

"I'm sorry," he said. "I must have said the

wrong magic word. I said: Sallylongsocks!"

Suddenly, Ms Fizz roared with laughter.

"Sallylong...SOCKS?" she chuckled. "Oh Cosmo!"

Cosmo looked up. Ms Fizz was smiling.

"It's not the end of the world," she said. "Come

here and I'll tell you the correct magic word."

Cosmo hurried towards Ms Fizz. She bent down and whispered in his ear. He waved his wand. "SALLYLONGSHANKS!" he said.

Flash! Bang! Crackle! Hiss! Sizzle!

The Little Green Monster disappeared in a puff of yellow smoke. There sat a little mouse. The mouse squeaked at Cosmo. Then it flicked its tail and scampered away.

"Thank you," Cosmo said as he swept up the rest of the stars.

"Everyone makes mistakes from time to time," said Ms Fizz. "But you did well second time round. I can tell that you'll be an excellent wizard."

"You have passed your Wizard Test," said Ms Fizz.

"So I am going to let you become a wizard."

Cosmo jumped for joy.

"Thank you," he said. "I will always try hard and do my best!"

Quiz

1. What does Cosmo want to be?

a) A monster

b) A wizard

c) A cat

2. Where is Cosmo's first test written?

a) On a toadstool

b) On a cupboard

c) On a toothbrush

3. What is the magic word?

a) Abra-kadabra!

b) Sallylongshanks!

c) Whizz!

4. What does the Little Green Monster tip over on Ms Fizz's desk?

a) A pot of pens

b) A hairbrush

c) A pot of glittery stars

5. Which animal does the monster turn into in the end?

a) A mouse

b) A dog

c) A hippo

Turn over for answers

Book Bands for Guided Reading

The Institute of Education book banding system is a scale of colours that reflects the various levels of reading difficulty. The bands are assigned by taking into account the content, the language style, the layout and phonics. Word, phrase and sentence level work is also taken into consideration.

Maverick Early Readers are a bright, attractive range of books covering the pink to white bands. All of these books have been book banded for guided reading to the industry standard and edited by a leading educational consultant.

To view the whole Maverick Readers scheme, visit our website at
www.maverickearlyreaders.com

Or scan the QR code above to view our scheme instantly!

Quiz Answers: 1b, 2a, 3b, 4c, 5a